BEFORE THE STORY STARTS, A POEM WRITTEN FROM THE HEART

IT'S NOT ALL MEN..

"IT'S NOT ALL MEN!" THEY SAY!
"I'D NEVER HURT A WOMAN, OK?!"

YOU'RE RIGHT, IT'S NOT ALL MEN
BUT, MOST OF THE TIME IT IS A MAN HURTING WOMEN

SNAPPING PICS UP THE SKIRT OF A WOMAN SHOPPING FOR SAUCEPANS,
IT'S NOT ALL MEN, BUT IT IS A MAN

VERBAL ABUSE DAILY, SHE WANTS TO LEAVE BUT DOESN'T FEEL LIKE SHE CAN
IT'S NOT ALL MEN, BUT IT IS A MAN

ATTACKED AT NIGHT, GETTING HOME SAFE IS THE PLAN
IT'S NOT ALL MEN, BUT IT IS A MAN

A SCHOOL GIRL WALKING HOME, CAT CALLED BY A VOICE FROM A VAN
IT'S NOT ALL MEN, BUT IT IS A MAN

TOO DRUNK TO CONSENT, TOO SLEEPY TO SAY THEY CAN
IT'S NOT ALL MEN, BUT IT IS A MAN

ASSAULTED AT WORK, DECLINED HIS ADVANCE
IT'S NOT ALL MEN, BUT IT IS A MAN

CONSCIOUS OF YOUR SURROUNDINGS, DONE MULTIPLE SCANS
IT'S NOT ALL MEN, BUT IT IS A MAN

HEARING STEPS BEHIND YOU, YOU WALK AS FAST AS YOU CAN
IT'S NOT ALL MEN, BUT IT IS A MAN

ABUSED IN YOUR HOME, RING ON YOUR HAND
IT'S NOT ALL MEN, BUT IT IS A MAN

PERSUADED TO STAY HOME WITH THE KIDS, NO INDEPENDENT FINANCE
IT'S NOT ALL MEN, BUT IT IS A MAN

SEEMED FUN AT FIRST. NOW I NEED TO SAY 'NO!' - I DON'T FEEL LIKE I CAN
IT'S NOT ALL MEN, BUT IT IS A MAN

SUCCESSFUL CAREER, AWARD WON, IT ALL WENT TO PLAN
HE WAS ALWAYS MY NUMBER 1 FAN
BUT NOW, I LAY BREATHLESS, I LEARNED FIRSTHAND
IT'S NOT ALL MEN, BUT IT IS A MAN

IT'S THE ONES YOU TRUST WITH YOUR LIFE
THAT CAN REALLY STICK IN THE KNIFE
OR THE ONES YOU DON'T KNOW AT ALL
THAT WILL LEAVE YOU LIFELESS, SPRAWLED

IN THE WOODS, IN THE DARK OR HOME ON THE FLOOR
EYES CLOSING, YOU HEAR YOUR KIDS CRY FOR
"MUMMY! IS MY MUMMY OK?"
"MUMMY WAKE UP, PLEASE STAY!"

WHO CAN WE TRUST?
WHEN WE HAVE TO TEACH OUR DAUGHTERS HOW TO ADJUST
AND LIVE THEIR LIVES DIFFERENTLY, JUST TO BE SAFE
WHEN WE HEAR THE NEWS, REPORTING CASE AFTER CASE AFTER CASE...

SO, NO, IT'S NOT ALL MEN THAT HURT US
BUT IT'S NEARLY ALWAYS A MAN,
DISCUSS...

WRITTEN BY JEN JENIVIVE

AND NOW THE STORY OF
MAN VS BEAR

BETTY AND SUE HAD A CHAT ONE FINE DAY, 'BOUT MEN VERSUS BEARS, IN A CURIOUS WAY.

"WELL, BEARS CAN EAT YOU!" BETTY DECLARED.
"A MAN'S LESS OF A THREAT," SHE FIRMLY COMPARED.

NEXT DAY, BETTY SET OFF, THE SUN
SHINING BRIGHT,
A WOODLAND WALK IN THE MIDDAY LIGHT.

SHE STROLLED DOWN THE PATH, HUMMING A TUNE, ENJOYING THE BIRDS AND THE FLOWERS IN BLOOM.

A STRANGER PASSED BY WITH A NOD AND A GRIN,
"HELLO THERE," HE SAID, WITH A WAVE, NOT A SIN.

AS THE SUN SET LOW, THEY LAUGHED AND THEY ATE,
BETTY AND BEAR, WHAT AN UNLIKELY FATE.

"GUESS I WAS WRONG," BETTY SAID WITH CHEER,
"OF ALL IN THE WOODS, I'M GLAD YOU WERE HERE."

THE END

About The Author
Jen Jenivive

Chooses the bear. Let's never stop talking about violence against women!

@jenjenivivereads

@jenjenivivereads

@jenjenivive

www.jenjenivive.com

Adult Parody Titles Include:

For full book collection visit www.jenjenivive.com

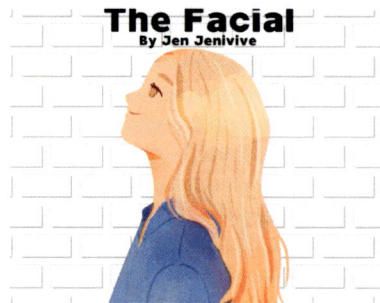

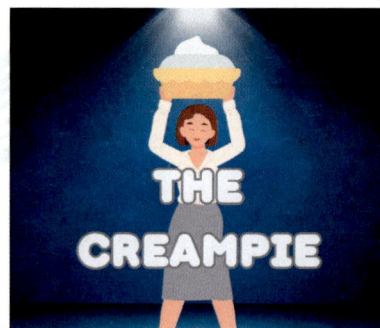

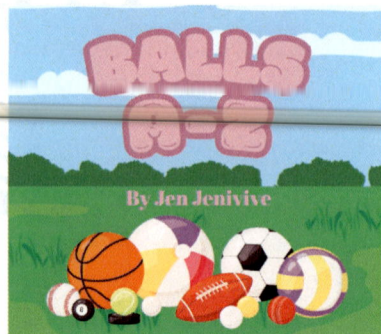

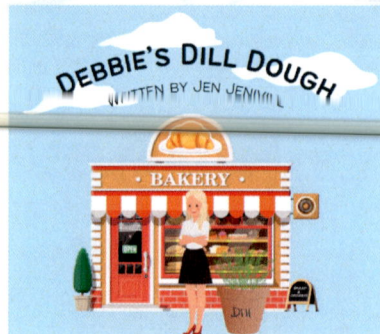

Flicking The Bean

The Facial
By Jen Jenivive

KELLY'S KEBAB
BY JEN JENIVIVE

Mums Great Tits
By Jen Jenivive

THE CREAMPIE

Good Girl
By Jen Jenivive

BALLS A-Z
By Jen Jenivive

DEBBIE'S DILL DOUGH
WRITTEN BY JEN JENIVIVE

BAKERY

Uncle Joe's Hoe

Made in United States
Orlando, FL
15 July 2025